Love Eternal

Colin Anderson

Ukiyoto Publishing

All global publishing rights are held by

Ukiyoto Publishing

Published in 2023

Content Copyright © Colin Anderson

ISBN 9789358465518

All rights reserved.
No part of this publication may be reproduced, transmitted, or stored in a retrieval system, in any form by any means, electronic, mechanical, photocopying, recording or otherwise, without the prior permission of the publisher.

The moral rights of the author have been asserted.

This is a work of fiction. Names, characters, businesses, places, events, locales, and incidents are either the products of the author's imagination or used in a fictitious manner. Any resemblance to actual persons, living or dead, or actual events is purely coincidental.

This book is sold subject to the condition that it shall not by way of trade or otherwise, be lent, resold, hired out or otherwise circulated, without the publisher's prior consent, in any form of binding or cover other than that in which it is published.

Dedication

Contents

Prologue	1
A Night To Remember	2
Catching Feelings	8
Dangerous Game	14
Screaming In Silence	23
Getting Even	29
Brief Encounter	37
Reunion	43
About the Author	50

Prologue

*I*nside a dimly lit apartment sitting at a wooden desk, sits a beautiful woman. Holding her head up with one hand, looking over a photo album, sobbing uncontrollably. Mascara running down her face. She tries to speak through her pain

Woman

(Crying)

Why.... why did you get in that fucking damn car? You knew she was a psycho.... I miss you so much Katie.... why?... just... why!

A ghostly image of a woman in a white dress, one half of her face is deteriorating, the other pristine... trying to call out, but to no avail. All of a sudden. The woman chuckles slightly.

Woman

Remember, where we met? Yeah course you do... Kupid's....

A Night To Remember

The image of the apartment swirls and changes to a very classy night club. Sitting at the bar is Katie. Dressed in a white top and skinny jeans and ankle boots. The owner Kelly is casually dressed with blonde hair, shaved at one side and make up. Walks up and pours Katie a drink, who in turn downs it in one. Kelly refills the glass.

Kelly Tyler

Bad day babe?

Katie Russell

You could say that... I've just finished with... now my ex girlfriend

Kelly Tyler

Aww babe, that sucks! You know your aunt Kelly will always be here for you.

Katie smiles weakly.

Katie Russell

(Chuckles Slightly)

Still sounds weird, when you say that.

Kelly Tyler

Your still my niece even though I'm married.

They both share a brief laugh. A scuffle in the corner of one of the booths catches Kelly's eye.

Kelly Tyler

HEY! NOT IN MY HOUSE YOU DON'T!

Kelly quickly marches to deal with the two men arguing and trying to hit each other.

Katie doesn't react, just swirls her glass, staring at it. A voice catches her off guard.

Woman

That glass won't drink itself.

This shakes Katie from her thoughts, turns to face the woman. She is tall, dyed two shades of pink, wearing makeup, long hair, brown eyes and dressed in a sleeveless white top, blue jeans and black boots.

> Woman
>
> Mind if I join you?

> Katie Russell
>
> (Disinterested)
>
> Sure... It's a free country.

The woman sits next to Katie, she motions to the bartender two drinks. She nods in response.

> Woman
>
> What's a pretty lady, like you doing in a place like...

> Katie Russell
>
> (Sarcastically)
>
> This? That line is so cheesy.

The bartender places the two drinks down. Katie hands over $20 but she wags her finger and chuckles. Katie places it back in her pocket.

Woman

(Curiously)

What was that?

Katie Russell

My aunt owns this place, I get free drinks. Even though I try to pay for them, and to get in.

Woman

Looks like you've got the golden ticket.

The slowly burst into laughter. Several hours later the two of them are more relaxed and chatting.

Katie Russell

So you got a name?

Rene Fernando

Rene Fernando, my parents are French and Hispanic.

Katie Russell

(Purrs Slightly)

Oh la la!

Rene Fernando

Oh very funny. So... wait... hold on. Your... the daughter of Dean Russell... the billionaire tycoon.

Katie Russell

(Whispering)

Shut the fuck up! Yes it's true, but I don't want the whole fucking world to know. Before you ask, yes my aunt knows. She doesn't treat me like some spoiled bitch.

Rene Fernando

(Sheepishly)

Sorry!

Katie Russell

(Calming Sigh)

You... didn't know...

Hours fly by as the club lights cut out as the main lights come on.

Kelly Russell

RIGHT YOU GUYS... MOVE IT!

The revellers quickly make there way to the exits. Rene and Katie get up to leave, but Kelly motions them to stay put. They flirtatiously softly touch each other, not knowing one of the revellers is watching....

As they exit Kupid's, it's the early hours of the morning. Rene hails s cab. And the person who was watching them stands and stares.

End of Chapter One

Catching Feelings

The sun slowly shines through the blinds. It catches Katie's smudged makeup on her face. She groans, turning over. She unintentionally hugs Rene. She wakes up in shock. Rene smiles and purrs.

>Rene Fernando
>Morning cutie.

>Katie Russell
>(Confused)
>How... did... you...

>Rene Fernando
>We agreed to me crashing here.

>Katie Russell
>(Slightly Annoyed)
>Yeah, on the couch!

> Rene Fernando
>
> Yeah well... the bed looked comfy, and you just looked so fucking adorable
>
> (Blushing Slightly)
>
> Th...thanks.

Rene fluidly gets out of bed, only wearing a thong. She slightly turns and notices Katie mesmerised. She gives a little wiggle and chuckles.

> Rene Fernando
>
> You like what you see?

> Katie Russell
>
> (Blushing)
>
> Oh... um.... I...

> Rene Fernando
>
> (Laughs Heartily)
>
> You can look, it's ok.

> Katie Russell
>
> Sorry!

Rene Fernando

All those sessions at the gym, are paying off.

She sits back on the bed, caressing Katie's face.

Katie Russell

I know that look, you want to know about... her..

Rene Fernando

What I... oh... if you don't want to, I understand.

Katie Russell

It's ok, I want to... her name is jade. Yeah she was lovely, in the beginning but... as time went on... it was like someone flipped a switch. She became... obsessed with me. Every where I went... boom... there she was... it was cute at first, but eventually it was pissing me off.

Rene Fernando

You said, right ok I get it. Now stop... hopefully she got the hint.

Katie Russell

It did stop... for a day, then the cycle would begin again. The final straw was... when she would follow me into the bathroom, and watch me pee.

Rene Fernando

(Disgusted)

Ew! Man that's gross, clearly she's never heard of privacy.

Rene stands quickly and paces the room angrily.

Rene Fernando

That fucking low life bitch, I'll kill her.

Katie Russell

Don't! I don't need that bullshit, back in my life. She thought I was cheating with guys. All because I'm bisexual... I prefer women to men.

Rene Fernando

For you... I won't... for now.

She climbs back into the bed and hugs Katie tight... They both fall asleep. Rene wakes up groggily and goes to the bathroom. The door bell rings just as she's finished. She walks to the front door and peers through the peep hole. She opens the door a little as the safety latch is on.

>Rene Fernando
>Can... I help you?

>Woman
>Is Katie in?

Rene realises who it is but remains calm.

>Rene Fernando
>(Sarcastically)
>You must be the infamous jade.

>Jade Rhodes
>Who the fuck are you?

>Rene Fernando

Me? I'm her new girlfriend! I treat her better, than the way you did.

Jade Rhodes

N...no, she's my girlfriend! Still is...

Rene Fernando

(Laughs Sarcastically)

You dumb bitch! She broke up with you...

Jade Rhodes

No we didn't, we're on a break.

Rene Fernando unbolts the door, and joins jade in the corridor, gently closing the door. She's wearing a sleeveless tank top. Jade notices her muscles and a military tattoo....

Rene's eyes narrow and stares at jade.

Rene Fernando

(Calm)

That's right bitch, don't... fuck... with... a marine. You come here again, I'll kick your fucking ass.

End of Chapter Two

Dangerous Game

It is early morning. Katie is in the local gym, stepping off the treadmill. Her face and top half of her body dripping with sweat. We follow as she heads to the lockers, opening hers to take a drink of her cold water. She lets out a satisfying sigh, and closes her locker. She is startled by jade standing there.

> Jade Rhodes
> Hi... hi babe.

> Katie Russell
> (Sarcastically)
> Really?

> Jade Rhodes
> Your still my babe...

> Katie Russell
> Your not my gf anymore, jade. Clearly the restraining order doesn't mean shit to you.

> Jade Rhodes

That's just a bit of paper, babe.

> Katie Russell
> (Shouting)
> I'M NOT YOUR FUCKING BABE.

Jade and the other onlookers are shocked. Katie storms out grabbing her kit back. Jade runs after her.

> Jade Rhodes
> (Pleading)
> Please babe, I'm sorry... I'll change. We can start again.

> Katie Russell
> (Angrily Crying)
> No jade, you wont. You think I'm going to fall for your bullshit and play happy families.?

Katie looks jade dead in the eye.

> Katie Russell
> (Emotionally Calm)

I'm only going to say this once... leave... me... the fuck... alone... were over... period!

Katie hurriedly heads to her apartment, she easily manages the stairs, quickly opens the door. Quickly entering her apartment and slams the door and dead bolting it. She slides down the door and sits in a fetal position. Sobbing uncontrollably. A gentle tap emanates from the door. Katie believes it's jade.

Katie Russell

Fuck off you psycho... BITCH!

Rene Fernando

Katie? Katie it's me.

She quickly unbolts the door, flinging it open, and tightly hugs her. Rene easily picks her up, carrying her inside and rebolts the door. Katie doesn't let go as she carries her into the bedroom. Rene sits down with Katie crying uncontrollably in her arms.

Rene Fernando

Baby, its ok... I'm here. Your safe now... let me guess... jade!

Katie nods. Then looks slowly up at Rene.

Katie Russell

She... she followed me to the gym.... I was SO fucking angry. She's got it in her thick head, we're still an item.

Rene Fernando

And the restraining order you told me about, meant jack shit then.

Katie Russell

Yup, but I think I've made it worse.

Rene Fernando

How so babe?

Katie Russell

I told her to her face, were over.

Rene Fernando

As a former commander in the marines, I know her M.O... she's delusional, quick to make rash decisions... acts on impulse. Her consciousness is telling her, that you never split. Her subconscious however, is telling her otherwise. But she's ignoring it.

Katie Russell

I know what she's like, when's she's told no... she will go all out.

Rene Fernando

I'll protect you, black belt In defence and all that.

They both share a hug as the image of them wisps and changes to Katie exiting a nearby supermarket. It unexpectedly starts to rain hard. She curses under her breath in frustration. We hear a car horn beep as a red Pontiac Firebird rolls into view. Katie freezes as she knows the owner. Jade rolls the window down automatically.

Jade Rhodes
(Shouting)
Get in. I'll give you a lift.

Katie Russell
(Shouting Back)

I'm not falling for your tricks, jade. I'd rather suffer the indignity of...

Jade Rhodes

And risk getting sick? I promise, I'll take you... home. Scouts honour.

Katie thinks for a moment, debating internally to herself, instantly deciding to take a chance and runs and jumps into the passenger seat.

Katie Russell

Look... I know I've been kinda harsh on you...

Jade Rhodes

It's... OK... I'll drive you... home.

Katie is slightly unnerved by the way jade is acting, but shrugs it off. There is a long awkward silence as they pull into a local gas station. By this point Katie has fallen asleep, exhausted. Jade fills up a gas canister, Eerily humming a non existent tune. She walks back to the car, staring intensely at Katie. For a brief moment she contemplates her actions. But she snaps out of it and gets in and drives off.

After many hours of driving. Jade pulls into a secluded part of a unknown forest. Katie is awakened by jade slamming the door hard. She looks at the setting sun, the sky a orangey glow. She tries to get out but she's tied up.

Jade returns opening her door. Smiling creepily

>Katie Russell
>
>Wh .. where am I?

>Jade Rhodes
>
>Nowhere they'll ever find you.... babe!

>Katie Russell
>
>Jade? Your not going to kill me, are you babe?

>Jade Rhodes
>
>(Emotionless)
>
>If I can't be your girlfriend, then this... Rene can't have you... see ya... babe!

We are a short distance away as we watch jade dump the gas inside of the canister all over the car and splashing Katie. We hear Katie begging, as she slams the door shut and locking it. Deliberately leaving the window down slightly, as she is taking out a box of matches. Striking one up and simultaneously lighting the rest. And pauses for a second, then tosses them into the car.

The interior quickly goes up in flames as we hear Katie's blood curdling screams as she is being burned alive. Jade watches smiling, then to regret and runs off as Katie eventually stops screaming. Two hours later the car is a mere charred smoking shell, a ghostly image of Katie with half her face burned, walks slowly forward, a soft light beams down. She looks skyward.

Katie Russell

(Distorted Ghostly Voice)

I know you mean well, and you want me to... I can't... not now.... jade has to answer for this... I only want justice to be served... all I ask is for a little time...
Please...

The beam fades as white orbs surround her., as a brief glow emanates from her.

Katie Russell

I'm grateful... I promise, once I've seen jade pay. I know you don't condone violence or revenge, but I want to her to suffer the same treatment, as she did when were together.

A lonely star appears in the night sky and flashes briefly then disappears. Katie smiles briefly

>Katie Russell
>I truly appreciate this, honestly...
>Wish me luck.

Katie floats off and phases through the trees and heads for home.

<u>End of Chapter Three</u>

Screaming In Silence

It has been several days since Katie's disappearance. Two officers are talking to Rene at the scene of the crime, who breaks down crying. Suddenly Kelly comes rushing in and instantly hugs Rene tightly, as the officers leave. They both look at the charred remains of the car. The ghost of Katie watches on.

Kelly Russell

(Crying)

Why... just... she never harmed anyone...

Rene Fernando

(Sobbing)

I wish... I went with her...

Kelly Russell

You didn't know this would happen sweetie, don't blame yourself.

Katie keeps her distance, watching.

Katie Russell

None of us did, how could I been so... blind

A voice catches her off guard.

Voice

Not blind, just didn't see the signs.

She turns to see a man in a suit and a cane. He bows respectfully.

Man

My apologies miss Russell... allow me to introduce myself... I am... Ronald...

Katie turns back to watch.

Katie Russell

Been told to keep tabs?

Ronald

On the contrary, more... advisement. If you wish to act... may I suggest you do it soon... otherwise...

Katie turns back and glares.

Katie Russell

Otherwise what...Ron! I'll be stuck here? You know what... she did.... all of this because I fell in love with... Rene.

Ronald

My deepest apologies miss Katie. That wasn't my intent... I know how exactly, the pain your experiencing... you see... I was also...

Katie Russell

(Softly)

Who hurt you?

Ronald

(Emotionally)

My... so called husband... yes... you heard that right, I'm gay... but love is love no matter what shape or form it comes in... you cant stop it..

Katie Russell

I agree, Rene was so kind to me... jade on the other hand...

Ronald

She has a warped sense of reality, only seeing what she wants to... I know her upbringing, doesn't justify her treatment of others... but... her version of love is... misunderstood... She sees things through rose tinted glasses.

Katie Russell

She was envious of me and Rene. She only wanted me for herself, no one else... wait... was she?... watching us that night we met?...

Ronald

I'm afraid so... she had been watching the two of you, all evening... jealous of the fact you were moving on, while she struggled with having no one to love. Which had triggered... events.

Katie Russell

Killing me, made the... situation a whole lot.. worse...

Ronald

I'm afraid so, I'm surprised you haven't seen her... since...

Ronald snaps his fingers and they reappear inside a dilapidated small apartment. Jade is sitting on a dirt stained deflated mattress. She is internally reliving her actions. The both them stand next to her.

Ronald

After... your untimely... departure...his is her current... state

Katie clenches her fists, shaking in anger reliving her own death while glaring teary eyed at jade. Unbeknownst to her the empty cans on the floor begin moving in time with her fists. Jade stares in total shock. Katie eventually calms and the cans abruptly stop.

Katie Russell

Did... I.... just...

Ronald

Yes you did, impressive... I know what your thinking... but quickly resorting to anger to manipulate objects WILL be taxing... but I can teach you...

Katie leans into jade's ear.

Katie Russell
(Eerily Whispering)
See ya soon... babe!

Jade shudders as the two of them disappear.

End of Chapter Four

Getting Even

Katie and Ronald are standing in the mists of limbo. Katie is slightly curious of her surroundings.

Ronald

To answer your burning question, yes we are in limbo at present.

Katie Russell

Why here?

Ronald

Out of sight, out of mind... The powers that be... are turning a blind eye to your actions. But they completely understand.

Katie Russell

So... what now?

Ronald

As you know, through concentration you will be able to manipulate objects. I must stress that being enraged, will quickly tire you out. All it requires is...

Katie Russell

Concentration. If I want something to move, I must focus on what object I want to be moved.

Ronald

You learn quickly miss Katie... or is it the fact you have watched a lot of paranormal... programmes?

Katie Russell

I have, but this is isn't going to be a walk in the park. If I want to REALLY scare jade, I have my work cut out...

Katie senses Rene's loneliness, and is quickly drawn to her, much to Ronald's surprise. Rene is sitting on Katie's bed hugging her favourite hoodie. Inhaling her scent from time to time, all the while crying uncontrollably. Katie tries to sit on the bed but phases right through cursing internally. She reluctantly stands beside her.

Katie Russell

Its going to be fine babe, I'm right here... I'll always be here for you.

A calming aura emanates from Katie, and it instantly sooths Rene. She tucks herself under the covers and falls asleep, exhausted. Ronald finally appears beside her.

Ronald

So this is...

Katie Russell

Shh!

Ronald

She can't hear us...

Katie Russell

I don't give a crap, I've just put her to sleep.

Ronald

Ahhh ... I must say, I'm truly impressed by your... development...

Katie Russell

All I did was say I was here for her.

Ronald

Which in turn, your calming presence had a positive effect on her

Katie Russell

It just comes naturally, I think...

Ronald

It does...

He looks at his pocket watch, then closes it.

Katie Russell

Something wrong?

Ronald

Our time together, has come to a... abrupt end... I'm afraid... it has been my pleasure miss Katie... I wish you the very best with your endeavour. And one more thing... karma can be a **very** vengeful lady...

He bows respectfully and dissipates into thin air. Katie looks at Rene smiling. For a moment she forgets what jade did, then is instantly reminded. She wills herself to appear in jade's apartment. She then disappears and then reappears in jades apartment. Katie is angered by the sight before her. Jade is kissing a unknown woman. She listens as jade calls this woman babe.

Katie watches on and after some time, decides she's had enough, waiting for this woman to leave. Eventually she does and jade is handed her number on a piece of paper. Soon as the door is closed, jade laughs as she rips it to little pieces. From nowhere a empty can slaps her hard in the face.

Jade Rhodes
What the fuck?

Two more cans also hit her in the face.

Jade Rhodes
What the hell?... who's doing that.

A eerily voice echoes in her mind.

Eerie Voice
(Singing)

Jade... oh jade... where are you babe!

Jade looks for where the voice is coming from. She eventually turns to search the bathroom, as she does a horrifying ghostly version of Katie lunges towards her, letting out a blood curdling scream. Jade backs off quickly and hits the wall slides down and sitting in fear as Katie just floats there. Several tense moments pass before Katie speaks.

Katie Russell

(Horrifying Voice)

THIS IS YOU'RE FAULT!

Jade Rhodes

(Scared)

K... Katie?... I'm...

Katie Russell

(Angered)

SORRY? FOR WHAT! MURDERING ME? ALL BECAUSE I FELL IN LOVE WITH RENE...

Katie's eyes glow a bright blood red, as she points at jade.

Jade Rhodes

You wouldn't hurt me... would you babe?

The mirror behind Katie breaks into pieces. They momentarily hover behind her. Then quickly phase through her as they slam into wall hard. Katie keeps one behind as jade winces. She looks at Katie as the last one whizzes by her face, leaving behind a large gash on her cheek. Blood trickles down from the open wound.

Jade Rhodes

Why are you haunting me, I...

Katie Russell

IM NOT GOING ANYWHERE, UNTIL YOU HAND YOURSELF IN. I HAVEN'T FORGOTTEN ABOUT YOUR LOVER EITHER...

Jade Rhodes

Please... don't hurt her, she's not part of this.

Katie reverts to her normal ghost form, and whizzes quickly towards jade and gets close to her face.

Katie Russell

(Softly)

Your nothing but a user jade, once you've got what you want... you toss them aside.

Jade Rhodes

(Sarcastically)

You didn't seem to mind.

Katie Russell

(Calmly)

Careful with that lying tongue of yours....

<u>End of Chapter Five</u>

Brief Encounter

Rene is standing at Katie's graveside, placing a bunch of beautiful flowers, dressed in black. She stands back up, staring at the head stone in silence. A middle aged man is at the next graveside beside her, they both unintentionally look at each other and smile. The man tips his hat in her direction. Katie watches on.

Katie Russell

(Mournfully)

Rene, I wish you could hear me...

The man looks up and notices her. Katie is stunned by this. He tips his hat in her direction. Rene blows the headstone a kiss as she is walking away. He beckons Katie to come closer. Katie drifts towards him.

Katie Russell

You... can see me?

Man

And hear you my dear.

Katie Russell

Who... are you?

Giles Baker

My apologies, I'm Giles Baker, and you must be Katie.

Katie Russell

I am, but how can you see and hear me?

Giles Baker

I have... the gift. You see... from a very young age I could see beyond the veil. At first yes, it was terrifying... eventually, over time I got used to it. My parents tried to commit me to a... mental institution...

Katie Russell

That's sad, especially you were a kid.

Giles Baker

Yes I was, the turning point was when I told my mother about her mother. I described her down to a t... my father thought I was.... possessed... but his great grandfather used my body to speak to him.

Katie Russell

Sorry for your loss.

Giles Baker

I appreciate the kind words, but my darling wife isn't in heaven..

Katie Russell

Oh.... I don't want to intrude, but....

Giles Baker

Unfortunately she was a cruel and vindictive woman. If any of the kids, or myself stepped out of line, then she'd lash out...

Katie Russell

She went down instead of up.

Giles Baker

Even though she was a vile cruel woman, I... still loved her. I prayed and hoped she'd see the errors of her ways, but fate had other ideas.

Katie Russell

Did you try and call to her?

Giles Baker

My presence, though welcome would upset the others. I did see her, but she just glared through me. I humbly requested to speak to her. I was granted a very brief moment.

Katie Russell

I take it was the latter...

Giles Baker

I'm afraid so, I was blamed for her being there. Why didn't I try harder... for the first time in my life, I stood up to her, and said that this was all her doing. She had no one to blame, but herself.

Katie Russell

She's in the perfect place then! I really am sorry, to watch your wife....

Giles Baker

(Chuckles Slightly)

Your kind words, warm this old heart. She can't haunt me either... which brings me to my next question. How are you able to manifest, for this long?

Katie Russell

It's... hard to explain but... where I died, kind of binds me here. And the fact I want to see my ex punished...

Giles Baker

I see your memories, oh... how horrible and disgusting your so called girlfriend... callously murdered you, all because you found some one better...

Katie Russell

She was jealous and possessive, only wanted me and me only....

Giles Baker

That doesn't constitute for murdering you. I deduce that, you asked for a little more... time to put your affairs in order. Unbeknownst to you that is why you're bound to your place of death. Which in turn allows you to manifest.

Katie Russell

Look... this is gonna sound... weird but,

Giles Baker

You require my help! I'd be honoured. Meet me at my house, where we will discuss matters.

End of Chapter Six

Reunion

Katie and Giles are in the cosy and welcoming living room. Pictures of his family and little ornamental lady's are everywhere. He is relaxing his comfy recliner while Katie stands.

Giles Baker

I know why you are standing. You fall through psychical objects.

Katie Russell

Yeah it's a pain in the ass...

Katie drifts to the window looking out at the farm. Giles smiles warmly and joins her.

Giles Baker

I feel your pain kid, really I do... but time is against you... I'm not saying that to rush you...

Katie Russell

I know your not, if I don't finish this... then I'll never leave.

Giles Baker

I've seen this time, and time again. Souls eternally bound here. I do my best to help them conclude there earthly business but, some do not wish to leave... which results in them being bitter...

Giles just stares out the window as we see spirits float aimlessly. Most of them notice Giles and smile, the others just ignore him.

Katie Russell

I won't end up like that. Being bitter, only makes you angry... which turns into resentment...

Giles Baker

I agree... but let's not dwell on that. I will guide you, as best as I can...

Katie Russell

So... where do we start?

The image wisps as it changes to the outside of the local P.D. Jade is seen being escorted out by a male detective. He grunts as he begrudgingly lets her go. As he heads back inside jade smiles smugly and sarcastically blows him a kiss.

Jade Rhodes

Bye sweetie...

Chuckling to herself as she walks off, but is caught off guard by the woman she was making out with earlier. Her smile quickly turns to disgust.

Woman

Hi baby...

Jade Rhodes

(Uninterested)

What do **you** want... Megan

Megan Dunst

Well silly, you never called me!

Jade Rhodes

Yeah well... you got too clingy, I don't that shit.

Megan Dunst

(Laughs)

Silly goose, you called me your babe, that makes me your girlfriend.

Jade starts to walk off but Megan grabs her arm, gripping it hard.

Jade Rhodes

Your... hurting me. Let me go!

Megan smiles madly, unsettling jade.

Megan Dunst

No I'm not silly, where do you think you're going?

Jade Rhodes

Err... Home!

Megan Dunst

Our... home silly...

Megan quickly and swiftly injects her with a syringe. She instantly falls unconscious. Hours later we see jade tied to a leather sofa. Eventually she comes round. Looking curiously at her surroundings. Megan comes back with a plate of freshly baked cookies, placing them down on jades lap. She kneels down and begins feeding them to her.

Megan Dunst

C'mon sweetie, you have to eat to keep your strength up....

Jade Rhodes

What do you want?

Megan Dunst

You... bitch! Just... you!

Megan's demeanour changes.

Jade Rhodes

Why? I don't even...

Megan Dunst

Me? Well you knew my sister, you fucking low life piece of shit.

Jade looks at Megan confused, as she gets close to her face, staring emotionless at her.

Megan Russell

(Coldly)

My surname isn't Dunst, that was just to confuse you... actually it's Russell...

Jade Rhodes

Your... her sister?

Megan Russell

Wow, I wonder what my... DEAD sister see in you... oh... I know... everything.

Jade Rhodes

So this is your plan? Kidnapping me! That's just... the most fucking dumb...

Megan punches her hard in the face.

Megan Russell
Shut the fuck up....

Jade Rhodes
(Wincing In Pain)
It'll... take more than that... bitch!

Megan Russell
(Chuckles)
Oh... I've got lots in store for you....

The End....?

About the Author

This is will be my first romance story... I'm sure you will enjoy.

www.ingramcontent.com/pod-product-compliance
Lightning Source LLC
LaVergne TN
LVHW041554070526
838199LV00046B/1964